SNOW

Uri Shulevitz

A Sunburst Book

Farrar Straus Giroux

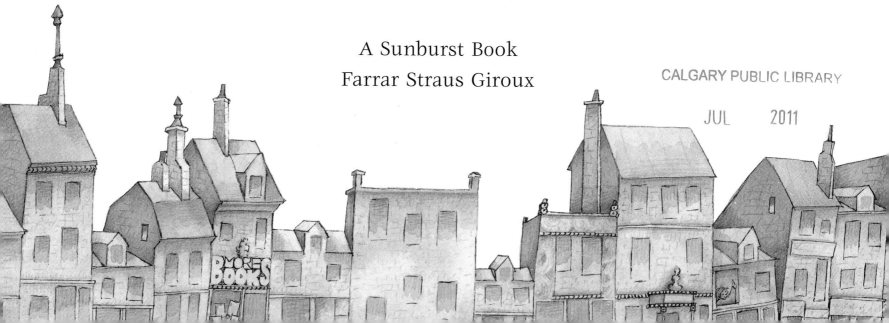

Copyright © 1998 by Uri Shulevitz. All rights reserved. Distributed in
Canada by Douglas & McIntyre Ltd. Printed in June 2010 in China
by South China Printing Co. Ltd., Dongguan City, Guangdong Province.
First edition, 1998. First Sunburst edition, 2004
16   15   14

www.fsgkidsbooks.com

Library of Congress Cataloging-in-Publication Data
Shulevitz, Uri, date.
     Snow / Uri Shulevitz.— 1st ed.
        p.   cm.
     Summary: As snowflakes slowly come down, one by one, people in
the city ignore them, and only a boy and his dog think that the
snowfall will amount to anything.
     ISBN: 978-0-374-46862-0 (pbk.)
     [1. Snow—Fiction.   2. City and town life—Fiction.]   I. Title.
PZ7. S5594Sn   1998
[E]—dc21
                                            97-37257

For
Margaret Ferguson

and for
Kiddo

The skies are gray.
The rooftops are gray.
The whole city is gray.

Then

one snowflake.

"It's snowing,"
said boy with dog.

"It's only a snowflake,"
said grandfather with beard.

Then
two snowflakes.
"It's snowing,"
said boy with dog.

"It's nothing,"
said man with hat.

Then
three snowflakes.
"It's snowing," said boy with dog.

"It'll melt," said woman with umbrella.

A few snowflakes float down
and melt.

But as soon as one snowflake melts
another takes its place.

"No snow," said radio.

"No snow,"
said television.

But snowflakes don't listen to radio,

snowflakes don't
watch television.

All snowflakes know
is snow, snow, and snow.

Snowflakes keep coming and coming and coming,

circling and swirling,
spinning and twirling,

dancing, playing,
there, and there,

floating, floating through the air,

falling, falling everywhere.

And rooftops grow lighter,
and lighter.

"It's snowing," said boy with dog.

The rooftops are white.

The whole city is white.

"Snow," said the boy.